MOON THRALL
by Mel Teshco

Moon Thrall
By Mel Teshco
Text copyright © 2015 Mel Teshco
All Rights Reserved

This is a work of fiction. Names, characters, places and incidents either are the product of the author's imagination or are used fictitiously, and any resemblance to actual persons, living or dead, business establishments, events or locales is entirely coincidental.

Cover Art by Kellie Dennis at Book Cover by Design
<u>www.bookcoverbydesign.co.uk</u>[1]

---

1. http://www.bookcoverbydesign.co.uk

Chapter One

The werewolf sank onto his belly among the tall, brittle grass, staying motionless and ever watchful as he peered over the rim of a fissured escarpment knotted with weeds. A log cabin some forty yards below sat smack bang in the middle of a bare paddock, scorched dry by a long gone Australian summer and a seemingly endless drought. Only a distant line of gum trees broke the desolation, framing the night sky like shadowy sentinels.

He shifted restlessly. His werewolf muscles, used to the flex and shift of a loping run, were stiff from his vigil that had seen him return here these last two nights. Beneath his thick black pelt his skin prickled with anticipation. The waiting was the hardest. Sheer willpower alone kept him frozen in place even when he was primed to explode from the thicket of yellowed grasses.

But there'd be no racing against fate. With the moon big and fat on the horizon, soon there would be no more waiting, no more hiding.

There were no signs of life inside the cabin. No lights broke the darkness, no television screen flickered. Not even a wisp of fireplace smoke lingered in the crisp winter air. A mortal would assume the dwelling was unoccupied. The werewolf knew better.

He slunk lower still in the tall, dry grass, whining low as his ears pricked forward, alert to the sudden movement inside the cabin. The woman, his *weren*, had awakened. Seconds later the door swung open. She appeared in the doorway, very much alone, the moonlight turning her long red-gold hair to flame. The werewolf's tongue slipped out, sweeping a semicircle around his whiskered muzzle. She looked surreal in her virginal, high-necked and long-sleeved sheer white dress.

The full moon lit up her slender silhouette and showcased the swell of her breasts, her almost flat belly and the dark triangle of her pussy between her thighs.

A growl rumbled deep in his chest, his belly tightening. But still he didn't move, though he could feel the vibrations of her emotions—anxiety, confusion, lust. The latter would intensify very quickly after her change, until every other sentiment would cease to exist, cease to matter.

He had hoped she'd come to realize she wasn't dreaming, hoped her subconscious would come to terms with her psyche long before she'd arrived here. But it was obvious she was clueless.

Most werewolf parents chose not to break the news to their children of their birthright, preferring they enjoyed a normal childhood—and indeed, for a short time, adulthood—for as long as possible. But in his experience, it was better a werewolf knew and accepted who they were well before their first complete transition on their twenty-fifth birthday. Well before the thrall of the full moon, and its sexual pull, overcame them.

Even now, unbeknownst to her, the male in him was stimulating her senses, inciting her change and a deep yearning for her wolf-mate. His hunger for her was twofold. He whined again, watching her stumble outside, her hands pressed to her belly.

He lifted his snout, scenting the air, tasting her pheromones. Need lanced straight to his loins, turning his whine into a barely restrained howl. But he would not approach her now. Her transition was almost upon her. The agony of change would, for a few minutes at least, override all else.

The woman abruptly flung back her head, the moonlight flooding her pale face. She spread her arms wide and laughed aloud, spinning like a top to a rhythm she had yet to understand.

His eyes narrowed, distorting the vivid abstract colors of his werewolf sight. It was time to make himself known.

Chapter Two

Elyse Wellston laughed again, the sound even more discordant and shrill. No surprise. She'd known these last few days she was going stir-crazy. Her emotions, which were already shot to pieces, had been seesawing right off the charts.

After close to five years of living with a possessive, carefully masked madman, she'd chosen now to break down? She was only glad Caleb, her monster of a fiancé—ex-fiancé—hadn't yet succeeded in tracking her down to witness her slide into insanity.

She swallowed. If she stuck to her plan, stayed solitary, invisible, she had at least half a chance to outmaneuver his far-reaching tentacles, his powerful influence.

Her belly cramped, much more painfully than what she'd experienced just minutes earlier. She bent over double. Laughter skidded into a strangled gasp, sweat beading on her forehead and upper lip. Pain, sharp and intense, exploded behind her eyes, a tunnel vision of swirling, too-brilliant colors. Her legs collapsed beneath her and she slumped to her knees with a groan, her throat convulsing, her skin rippling.

What is happening to me?

Further coherent thought fled. She heard the bones in her forearms crack almost simultaneously to her scream of pain, an agony that intensified and moved, seemingly growing. The muscles in her legs bunched, squeezing tight. And then her screams lost all volume as those same muscles tore apart, shredding under the intense pressure.

But it was only when the bones completely gave way, snapped like toothpicks before jagging into her flesh, that she came to understand the true concept of physical suffering.

She'd experienced more than her fair share of pain. A dislocated jaw, two broken fingers along with bruised and swollen eyes on more than a few occasions. Her fiancé's *loving* hands had also broken one of her wrists, two of her ribs and given her bruises and welts in too many places and too many times to recall.

But never had that pain equaled this.

At some distant place she heard a scream tear past the sudden loosening of her throat, heard her nightgown rend. Her jaw popped, her spine. She fell to her side, sniveling and whimpering between gasps of breath. Then as her backbone gave way, stretching and pushing, everything swirled in multicolor and abruptly went black...

She came to slowly, becoming aware of her physical changes yet strangely not frightened by them. Pain was all but forgotten, pushed aside as other, more significant things claimed her attention.

She wasn't human, and not just physically. Mentally she was different. Stronger and far more confident. She was...empowered. A pelt covered her skin, her four legs and...tail.

Scents overwhelmed her and she tentatively lifted her head, raising her snout to breathe them all in, one after the other. A dead carcass some distance away, pungent eucalyptus, pine, wattle and dust. And something not quite human. Something...virile.

Involuntarily, her long tongue slipped out and swept around her snout. Her ears flickered, swishing back and forth, hearing and discarding the hoot of an owl from far away, a lizard scampering through twigs and dry leaves. All her focus stayed on the almost silent stealth of approaching oversized paws.

When a rock tumbled and bounced down the cliff face close by, she struggled to get onto her feet—her paws. She staggered momentarily as she adjusted to the extra pair of limbs. Her vision blurred again, the black of the night wavering in and out until it finally became diamond bright with color, rippling and vibrating around her.

Her body tightened and tingled, the hair on her back—her ruff—standing high, long before the big black animal that was too big to be a wolf, emerged through the disjointed colors of her tunnel vision. She growled, terrified and mesmerized all at once.

The most primitive part of her recognized this beast was her male counterpart. His brilliant gray eyes turned molten, flashing red heat and causing her body—her new body—to respond like it was lit from within. On flat land now, he advanced in a ground-eating trot, his big body supple and powerful, his limbs long and muscled.

She lifted her snout with what seemed instinctive reflex, scenting his maleness, his lust. And incredibly, a yearning that had steadily escalated since her arrival here stirred deep within, pushing away the boundaries of her fear, her insecurities, to leave behind only the faintest residue of instilled human emotions.

She acknowledged in some distant part of her brain how easily she was leaving behind her old self. But as the male touched his nose to hers in greeting, she could no more fight against the beast instinct that governed her than she could the change that'd overcome her...electrified her.

Fire now filled her loins, sizzled through her veins like a drug until she almost writhed with need. They padded around each other, giving free rein to their senses. Then looking up to the moon, they released a long, discordant howl, one after the other.

A far off gunshot cut short their song. Elyse stiffened, her muscles trembling in preparation for flight or fight. The male werewolf whined, snuffling her face and letting her know she had nothing to fear. But when the second gunshot blasted closer still, she leapt forward, her long legs now working in perfect coordination, her huge paws barely touching the ground.

Long dry grass whipped her snout, wind whistling past her ears that were flattened close to her skull. Her tongue lolled out, breaths long and deep as her stride quickly ate up the miles.

She wasn't sure exactly when flight became foreplay, when fright became a challenge to keep one stride ahead of the male who all too easily loped behind. Fear had become something else entirely.

Something much...hotter.

She lurched to a stop on the edge of a cliff face, whining with recognition at seeing her cabin below. She'd come full circle. No, almost certainly the male had steered her that direction.

Beneath her fur coat she shivered, but she wasn't a bit cold. Red-hot lust poured through her veins, clambering for attention. And though her limbs were shaky with fatigue, the urge to mate was undeniable, unbearable.

She whimpered when sparks shot like acid firecrackers behind her eyeballs. Her bones shuddered, preparing to shift.

Oh, shit.

She scrambled away from the dangerous drop-off. *Too late.* Her hind legs collapsed beneath her, and in slow motion she felt herself falling and sliding backward, over the precipice.

A man shouted out her name a millisecond before his hands grasped great handfuls of her coat. She yelped as chunks of her fur tore free in his grip, and then, with the change bolting through her, she plummeted in a bone-jarring tumble all the way to the cliff base.

Long minutes later she lay motionless in her human form, the sheer agony of her broken body disabling all ability to move, to utter a sound. Rocks clattered far above, followed by a man's grunt of exertion as he scrambled down the cliff face.

She attempted to look up and view the man who had tried to save her. Pain instantly rebounded through her skull, lashing through her chest with every little breath, every heartbeat. *Fuck.* She was used to pain, but this...this was unimaginable torture.

Yet even through it all she sensed the man's arrival. He moved close and peered down at her, concern etched into every line of his dark, handsome face. He crouched, laying a gentle hand on her burning, sticky-wet face. "You need to change back into werewolf."

Werewolf?

She tried to talk, to deny the very idea. Instead she half-choked on the coppery tang of blood filling her mouth.

His eyes hardened, resolute. "You have to change now, or you won't survive."

Oh, hell. He was serious! She couldn't nod even had she wanted to, but something in her stare must have deciphered her acknowledgement. Her resignation. What other choice did she have?

"The thrall of the moon has passed, but it's possible for you to change back into beast form while the moon is full in the night sky." His voice was crystal clear within the terrible chaos of her hurt. "As werewolf you can heal." Determination glinted in his jade eyes. "But you have to allow the beast its freedom, coax it from hiding. Imagine it back to life."

She'd promised herself never to put her trust in another man ever again. But right then she had no choice. She had nothing—and everything—to lose. She envisioned herself as the creature she'd been.

Immediately the hair on the back of her neck stood up, along with the sensation akin to an army of ants crawling up and down her spine. Her back arched despite the intolerable pain. A scream built inside her throat as a savage trail of fire singed her innards and pulsed outward, searing her pores.

The man stepped back, out of range of the claws pushing through the crescents of her nails. "The pain will end soon."

She spat out blood with a gurgled cry, wishing then for the sweet mercy of death. When a curtain of darkness washed over her and blotted out all the pain, she slumped, sighing. The man had spoken the truth.

Chapter Three

Elyse woke with a start. Not again. She peered down at herself. She was naked and dusty, the ends of her long hair matted with dried blood, a crust of which covered much of skin with its cuts and grazes.

Where the hell had she been this time? What the hell had she done? She ached all over, but it was the unrelenting ache between her thighs that needed immediate attention.

One hand skating over the triangle of reddish-blonde hair along her pussy, she parted her labia and touched her plump clit. Her breath hitched at the immediate spark bolting through the sensitized nerve endings and she bent her legs and spread them apart, watching the rhythmic play of her fingers as she opened her cunt wider still and circled her clit, faster and faster.

A man with overlong dark hair appeared in her mind, and suddenly her hand was his mouth as he tasted her pussy, his tongue sucking her swollen clit. She gasped. A climax hit her hard, a short-lived and sharp sensation that left her immediately dissatisfied. An itch she was unable to give a good scratch.

She dropped her hands back to her sides. Self-stimulation wasn't nearly enough. Need had been snapping and snarling at her heels from the moment she'd run from her past and into this new life.

She sat upright, still fuzzy from lack of sleep. While she'd sleepwalked she'd managed once again to lose her clothes. Her very last set. She'd only grabbed a few changes of lightweight clothes to carry easily in her bag.

She closed her eyes, pressing a hand to head as she tried to recall anything from the night before. An ache immediately sprung to life behind her eyes, and she sighed, surrendering to the wooly blanket of her mind. "I'm really losing it," she muttered.

Would she ever discover her sudden need to sleepwalk each night? Did she want to? One didn't need to be a genius to guess escaping from an abusive man had released enough pent-up emotions to see her wander in her sleep.

Swinging her legs to one side of the bed, she paused to listen for a moment and scan the immediate area for any motion, any changes. It was a habit she didn't want to break anytime soon. For as long as Caleb lived, she'd never let her guard down, never imagine he'd give up finding her. His pride would demand recompense. His ego would demand respect.

She shivered a little, but sensing nothing amiss, she pushed to her feet, wrapping the sheet sarong-style around herself before wandering into the sparse, almost nonexistent kitchen. She didn't have a clock, but by the sun climbing high on the horizon she guessed it was late morning. Running on nerves, she rarely slept in. Yet, these last few days, what with the sleepwalking and the odd self-awareness throbbing between her thighs and heating her blood, she'd been lucky to wake before midday.

Smothering a yawn, she moved past the rickety table and couple of chairs—the only furniture aside from the squeaky old single bed—then pulled open the cupboard and peered halfheartedly inside. Coffee, sugar, tinned soup and a packet of unopened biscuits.

She'd lost her appetite from the first time Caleb had swung a punch her way. And none of his profuse apologies or declarations of love after each "episode" had managed to bring her appetite back. Perversely, when she'd lost her curves, she'd won his hard-to-gain approval.

Caleb had actually admired her new look. She'd apparently looked stunning on his arm at one meaningless black-tie event or another in her glittering, figure-hugging designer dresses. "Coffee it is," she said aloud, burying her musings before managing to smile wryly at this latest habit of talking to herself.

She lit the old gas camping stove she'd bought at a secondhand shop in town some three hours' drive away. She'd also bought a gas bottle and some carefully selected supplies, which included a light blanket and the single sheet that now doubled as a dress.

Staying as inconspicuous as possible, Elyse noticed an elderly male cashier had hardly glanced at her in the oversized knit jumper, black leggings and a beanie she'd stuffed every last strand of her fiery hair into. She shook her head, her lips twitching into another smile. Here she was, no car, no electricity and no phone. And she'd never felt more alive. More at home. More safe.

Using the back door, she hoisted up her ready-made "dress" and stepped outside to fill the copper kettle from the tap of a rusty galvanized water tank. She rapped on the corrugated rings, frowning at the hollow sound that rang out from within. Water was a precious commodity out here. The fact that there was any water at all proved no one had lived here for quite some time.

The tap squealed protest from too little use as she shut off the pressure. She chewed her bottom lip, steadying her nerves at the ensuing silence that seemed almost loud. She stilled, straining to hear anything unusual, anything at all.

"Get a grip." She slowly released the oxygen from her lungs, her shoulders loosening. Still, she couldn't stop a chill from seeping into her skin and slipping right into the marrow of her bones as she hurried back inside. Alert to anything and everything, she placed the kettle onto the gas flame and spooned a teaspoon of instant coffee into her chipped mug. She glanced over at her backpack that lay at the ready beside her bedroom door, filled with the barest of essentials.

She was prepared to leave this all behind if she caught even a whiff of Caleb anywhere near. She shook her head. "Yeah, I've got so much to lose by staying."

But instinct told her she really did have everything to lose if she up and disappeared. She'd been drawn here like a homing pigeon returning to its roost. Instinct...self-preservation—it'd been almost uncanny the force within that drove her here.

Finding this abandoned cabin had seemed like providence after she'd begged a ride with a pair of European travelers who were exploring the wide open spaces of Australia. The couple would have been long gone before Caleb or anyone else had a chance to find them and question them on her whereabouts.

Taking her mug of black coffee out the front door, she sank onto the third step at the top and lifted her face to the sun. If she'd learned one thing these last five years, it was that freedom could not be bought nor taken for granted. She knew Caleb would be coming for her. And his retribution would not be pretty.

She shivered, goose bumps prickling along her flesh. And as if in forewarning, she saw it—a yellow SUV in the distance—moving quickly toward the cabin...toward her, throwing up a plume of dust in its wake.

"Shit." Her mug dropped from nerveless fingers, bouncing onto the step and dashing scalding coffee across one half-exposed thigh as she scrambled to her feet and high-tailed it indoors. And that was as far as she got. Her fragile world crashing around her, she slumped to the floor, aware she'd left the door wide-open but beyond caring now.

Something was wrong, very wrong. Her belly cramped, her muscles, spasms that intensified as the car drew to a stop outside her open door. She fell to her side, facing the vehicle, gasping.

Yet even riddled with pain she couldn't fail to notice how the tall, dark-haired man alighted with such sinuous, fluid grace. The very same man she'd imagined minutes earlier, sucking and licking her pussy!

Her mind suddenly popped with vivid images, one after the other, flashes of clarity from too-real dreams—the approach of a large animal...wolf...beast. The inherent knowledge that she'd found what she'd been looking for—and a deep need to be with the beast, despite herself.

The vision dissolved when her body cramped doubly hard, her insides pulling a hundred different directions. Her breath whistled through clenched teeth. She couldn't move even as he silently appraised her, his gray-green stare roving over her. Cold. Clinical. Just like Caleb.

Her jaw unlocked as she jerked the sheet closer to her body. "Get. Away. From. Me." But her voice barely rose above a hoarse whisper.

His expression flickered as he moved forward, striding up the stairs before stilling above her. His towering body blocked out the daylight, his straight, almost black hair brushing his broad shoulders and framing his fierce, almost too-handsome face as he looked down at her, his brilliant eyes probing her face, reading her thoughts. "I won't hurt you," he said. She almost laughed. Almost. But her belly was roiling as her body continued to pull her innards every which way. "You shouldn't be experiencing this now, not in full daylight," he murmured.

"Unless—"

"I don't know...what you're...talking about," she said hoarsely, her vision swimming with unshed tears.

He frowned a little, then said, "Don't fight it. The more you do, the worse it gets." He crouched to her level, and even with the pain she flinched as he swept a lock of hair from her brow, his touch somehow familiar yet unexpectedly tender. His gaze held hers. "What you're fighting isn't just physical. You've yet to accept the truth. And your denial is tearing you apart. Literally."

She closed her eyes, trying to ride out the agony. It took perhaps a full minute before she asked with a croak, "Who are you?"

His thumb pad blotted a lone tear trekking down her cheek. "I'm your future," he said softly, reasonably.

Chapter Four

As quickly as the intense pain had come, it disappeared. But the ordeal had left her shaky and weak. To the point she could hardly form protest. And didn't.

His piercing eyes swept over her. "The pain shouldn't reappear now, not until tonight."

She didn't know or care how he knew this, but she believed him. "Is that supposed to make me feel better?" She felt his gentle hands on her thigh and guessed he wasn't about to reply when she heard his sudden sharp inhalation as he viewed the red, raised mark on her leg. And suddenly, unbelievably, she felt a whole different type of pain—and it was nothing to do with the burn.

"You've hurt yourself," he said roughly.

She managed a nod as his work-roughened fingers carefully outlined the red blotch on her thigh with its angry-looking blisters. How long had it been since someone had even half-cared she was hurting? Too damn long. She'd had a whole houseful of staff turn a blind eye and a deaf ear to the goings-on between Mr. Marsden and his fiancée interloper.

Their silence had been bought and paid for, not one of them stepping forward to offer a kind word let alone an offer of help from the nightmare she lived. She closed her eyes for a moment, hiding the effects of his touch.

He aroused much more than sentimental thoughts. She burned for him, wanted his hands on her, all over her. Heaven help her, she wanted him to fuck her now and to hell with the consequences!

"You need some cold water." He looked up with a frown as he noted her obvious lack of a kitchen and running water.

Pulling her mind out from between the sheets, she managed to croak, "It's not that bad," unsure if she meant her burn or the lack of amenities.

"Perhaps a cold cloth," he muttered. Not bothering to waste time looking for one, he stretched his arms over his head and pulled off his gray cotton T-shirt, exposing his lightly muscled abs and his golden chest with its sprinkling of dark hair. A knotted brown leather cord encircled his neck, its loose ends brushing just past his collarbone. "I'll be right back."

She managed a jerky nod at the sharp clench of need between her thighs, mesmerized by the sight of his naked torso, his all too masculine build. Less than a minute later he was crouched beside her and placing the improvised cold compress on her thigh. His eyes caught hers. "I hate to give you more bad news," he said gruffly, "but it seems I've used the last of your water."

She didn't answer straight away. What could she say? She'd been planning on staying here for a long time yet, sequestered away in the middle of nowhere. She snagged her bottom lip and gave a weary nod. So much for being drawn to this place...like being here was meant to be.

His brow furrowed. "I'm sorry. But you need water. And someone to look at your burn." He nodded toward his car. "There isn't a hospital close by, but I can drive you to the one-doc medical center in town."

"No." She managed a smile, though it made her jaw ache with the effort. "I-I came here for its isolation." A half-truth was better than a straight-out lie, surely. "And I'm really not in any mood for company right now," she said with a shrug, trying for casual but only too aware he wasn't fooled a bit.

His expression firmed. "Then you're coming to stay with me—at least until your leg is better."

Even as something forbidden rose up inside her—need, lust, yearning—a strong aftershock of denial immediately counteracted the feeling. "Absolutely not." The burn in her stare felt way fiercer than the one imprinted on her thigh, the fire in her soul shining right through. She would never cede control to a man again. Ever.

"Then I'm taking you into town. It'd take at least two days to walk there from here, probably more in your condition. And without water it'd be almost impossible."

Her shoulders slumped. He was right. She was being stubborn now, reckless. "Are there no other options?"

He turned the compress over, and a fresh wave of cool relief settled over her thigh as he said, "No. I'm afraid you're short out of those. It's the doctor in town. Or my place."

She closed her eyes, hiding the sudden, unexpected tears of frustration as much as the contrary, shameless lust filling her.

"I have a spare bedroom," he said hoarsely and all too gently.

Her lashes fluttering open, she nodded. Her instincts had become finely honed since she'd lived with Caleb and his many mood swings, yet they were even sharper now, extraordinarily so. To the point that she trusted this man, a total stranger, despite her obviously rampaging hormones and deep-seated fear factor. "Then I guess it's...your place."

God, she sounded so ungrateful. "Thank you."

Damn it, instincts or not, she shouldn't be feeling this weird sense of rightness with this stranger, of safety and belonging. But she did.

He nodded, a gleam of something—satisfaction?—in his stare. "Good." He stood. "You should rest your leg. I'll get your things."

As he headed to her kettle and gas stove, the long muscles in his honey-gold back shifting like fluid rope with every step, she croaked, "No." He turned to her and she explained, "I want to leave everything here."

When it rains I'll be coming back.

She swept a hand from out of her sheet folds, toward her bag, wishing she had at least one change of clothes still inside it—even one of her despised cocktail dresses. "Except that."

"Very well. I'll put your bag in the car while you dress."

She bit her lower lip. "I don't have any more changes of clothes."

"Ah." That one word made it seem almost as if he understood. She was even more grateful he didn't ask questions, which she wasn't sure how to answer. Instead he simply nodded and said, "I'm sure there will be something for you to wear at my home."

They didn't bother making small talk on the bone-rattling ride to his house, which she discovered was just a five-minute drive from the cabin she'd called home these last three days.

She perceived that he too felt the overwhelming awareness between them, a sensitivity that was almost surreal in its power. She felt his eyes on her time and time again, his sweeping glance undoubtedly taking in her erratic little breaths, her stiff profile, her clenched hands and rigid posture...her hard breasts with their even harder nipples poking through the white cotton sheet.

The tires were suddenly smooth underneath as they hit the long asphalt-sealed driveway. A double-storied red cedar house stood in all its glory at the end of the road, its corrugated iron roof gleaming silver under the late midday sun.

She turned to him, keeping her eyes—her rampant thoughts—above his bare torso. "You never told me your name."

He shifted down a gear, and she couldn't help but note the smooth flex-and-relax action of his biceps, his abdominal and shoulder muscles.

"Dane." A wry smile tilted one corner of his lips when he elaborated, "Dane Maddox."

"Dane Maddox, as in Maddox shipping?" She asked, feeling sheepish as soon as the words left her mouth. The Dane who owned Maddox shipping and realty, as well as countless other big businesses, would be decades older than the man she sat beside now.

The wry tilt of Dane's lips turned into a grimace before he asked, "You know him?"

"Not personally. Though I've heard all about him—hard not to, really—my ex-fiancé hated even hearing his name." Caleb had burned with resentment knowing he couldn't compete with the wealthy and very elusive Dane Maddox. "Odd really, considering that Dane doesn't appear to socialize like—"

"Like?" he prompted.

My ex-fiancé and his rich, crony hangers-on.

"Most celebrities."

"I guess not everyone feels inclined to flaunt their assets," Dane said with an offhand shrug.

Her belly lurched. Caleb was the master of conceited self-importance. His exquisite fiancée—the media's words, not hers—his ever-expanding bank balance, his investment portfolio... He loved to rub it all in the faces of those not to his measure. He strived to be the richest, the most influential and famous, despising anyone a notch higher than him. Maddox was many notches higher.

"Yes, you're right." Her face warmed. Dane's words reminded her she'd grown jaded in a world she'd barely endured living with Caleb. As Dane pulled beside the house and killed the engine, she said a little too huskily, "I want to thank you for coming to my rescue."

His gaze caught and held hers. "It was my absolute honor."

Silence thickened around them. And it seemed like minutes later, but it was likely only seconds, when she finally managed to formulate some words. "Can I ask you something?"

He nodded. "Sure."

"What made you go to the cabin this morning?"

His shrug was casual, but she noticed the clench of his smoothly shaven jaw when he said, "I knew you were there."

"You...did?" she squeaked.

He nodded, and though his glance was brief, she felt the possessive burn of his stare like a physical touch. "I've been expecting you," he said hoarsely.

What? Her heart thumping like a jackhammer, she asked, "You've been following me?"

His eyes flashed with some indefinable emotion. Then he was out of the car and thrusting the passenger door open. "Come, let's take a look at your burn."

He shouldered her bag as she clambered awkwardly out of the SUV. And once inside he added, "Make yourself at home while I grab the first aid kit."

A few minutes later she was sitting at his square timber table while he applied aloe vera burn cream to her thigh. She bit down on her bottom lip, caught between agony and ecstasy at his touch. He looked up from where he squatted before her, and she suddenly imagined taking hold of the leather cord encircling his throat and tugging him close, her lips melding to his while her tongue slid deep inside his mouth.

"Are you okay?" he asked.

Actually I'm horny as hell and want to fuck you senseless.

She licked her lips at such a lewd thought, and his gaze held hers as she croaked, "Yes."

Dane capped the lid, his lips pressed into a hard line.

Elyse swallowed, but not because he'd perceived her lie. She was too shockingly aware of his rippling washboard stomach, his dusky nipples and dark brown, almost black hair that feathered in a haphazard manner to his shoulders and which she wanted, desperately, to run her hands through. "I'll be fine."

"After tonight this will probably heal anyway," he murmured, half to himself.

"I've always healed quickly," she agreed, shuddering inwardly as she recalled just how soon Caleb had replaced one fading bruise with another. Of course, mostly he marked where people couldn't see. He would never be seen with anything less than a perfect woman on his arm.

Dane's stare once again held hers, his face thoughtful. Forcing a smile, she added, "But never that quickly."

He stood, stretching his body out with feline grace. "Then you might be surprised."

She dropped her gaze to the parquet floor. "Believe me, nothing much surprises me anymore."

The breath left her throat as his warm fingers cupped her chin, drawing her stare back to his. Unlike Caleb's, this man's touch wasn't repellent. She truly did want to be touched by him...to be held...kissed. And more. "Your eyes show many scars," he said softly. "You've lived much horror in your short life."

She quivered at his touch, his perception. He spoke of her psychological scars, not the physical. How he knew, she wasn't sure, and somehow she didn't much care. Not right then. A wanton need had taken hold deep inside and grew stronger with every second.

"I'm almost twenty-five," she whispered. "Still young, and yet I feel much older." She shook her head at his steadfast, too-knowing gaze. "I don't understand," she breathed. "You don't even know my name. We're strangers." She bit into her bottom lip, "Yet it doesn't seem to matter."

I never thought it'd be possible to feel this way about a man again.

"We're connected," he said, almost matter-of-factly, though his expression was intense, watchful. "You were drawn to me, compelled to find me."

She lifted her chin, feeling suddenly faint with...what? Expectation? Anticipation? "How is that possible?"

"You're my *weren*. My woman. Our coming together was inevitable."

My weren.

Like déjà vu the words echoed in her head, and though she didn't understand the term, it triggered something deep within. And for the first time in too long, there were no doubts or reservations. Logic and rational thinking didn't matter right then. It was just him and her, just the here and now.

She let out a sigh, the last of her fears dropping away like a serpent shedding its old skin and revealing the beautiful diamond pattern beneath. Primal, reawakened needs poured through her veins as she whispered starkly, "Make love to me."

His stare glowed with a strange animalistic light. Then he was leaning forward, pressing a tender, almost chaste kiss to her lips that left her wanting so much more. He pulled back with a deep, shuddering breath, and she was consumed by a need to have him take her mouth properly, to possess it.

Her heart flip-flopped. She was meant to be with him—of this she was suddenly, irrevocably certain. "Tell me you want me," she whispered.

"I want you," Dane said hoarsely. "God only knows I do. I want to make love to you over and over again." He dragged a hand through his hair. "But first, there's something you should know about me."

"A secret?" she asked weakly.

He nodded. "Of a sort."

She shook her head and put a hand up, stopping further explanation. "Don't. Not now. I have...I have secrets of my own." Secrets she didn't want to share. This would be her last night of pleasure before she'd leave. And as strong as she perceived Dane was, staying any longer would almost certainly mean his death.

Caleb would see to that.

She dug teeth prints into her lower lip. Tilting her head to one side, she said starkly, "Secrets I want you to make me forget."

Chapter Five

Something changed between them just then, a shared understanding, an agreement, a need that couldn't be denied. She didn't have to see the glint in his brilliant gray-green stare, didn't need to read the lust in every perfect line of his masculine body.

Her blood thrummed hot through her veins, pooling liquid heat between her thighs. She'd never felt this bold, this assured, this seductive. And as she parted the sheet draped around her body before dropping it to the floor, she realized she'd never felt this beautiful, either.

She didn't need designer clothes, expensive jewels and exquisite makeup to look like a million dollars. With just one glance, Dane made her feel like someone to be treasured and adored.

"So gorgeous," he murmured huskily. In one economical movement he stooped low, his mouth covering hers and his arms encircling her waist to pull her close.

Wow, she thought hazily. She belonged in his arms, could stay like this forever, dancing this incredibly slow dance that had them swaying, kissing as one to their own silent tune.

She pulled away, and looking up into his savage face stripped bare of all but the most fundamental emotions, she saw a tender reverence that left her awash with feelings she'd never experienced before. "Dane, I need you," she whispered.

His eyes sharpened, glowing with a possessive light. But she knew this man would never hurt her. Not physically, and never deliberately. She crouched to unsnap his jeans and unzip them before helping him out of the denim, followed by his boxer briefs.

His cock jutted hard and long, his chest rising and falling as though he couldn't quite catch his breath. She'd never enjoyed oral sex, but now, with this man, she craved it like never before. Clasping the base of his smooth, silken shaft, she took the head of his cock into her mouth and tasted his musky maleness.

He groaned, and a delicious thrill immediately bolted through her blood and sent her knees weak. She savored even more of his length, sucking up and down until his fingers were curling through her hair to urge her on, to keep her still.

"No more," he growled hoarsely.

She released him, basking in his near loss of control. Sweet heaven, she was close to falling off that same cliff edge herself! His skin tasted salty and a little bit woodsy as she pressed lingering kisses to the warm, lightly rippling plane of his abs.

Inhaling sharply, he drew her onto her feet and tilted her head up, recapturing her mouth with his.

She surrendered to him with a sigh, parting her lips as his tongue slid inside her mouth. It felt like seconds, but it was minutes later when he broke the kiss, their breaths heavy in the air.

She gasped surprise when he swept her up into his arms, and she clutched his broad shoulders, his strength so very apparent as he carried her up a steep staircase with effortless strides. He kicked the door open and she felt the rasp of a blanket on her bare back when he laid her on his bed.

His eyes never once left hers as he followed her down to kneel on either side of her thighs, careful not to brush against her burn. She held his stare, aware her eyes reflected the carnal heat rushing to her cunt when the tip of his erection slid along her slit, her plump, sensitized clit.

"I've been waiting for this moment for so long," he said hoarsely. "So very long."

She swallowed back a moan. "I think maybe I have too."

Sex with Caleb had been just that: sex. A quick, mostly one-sided fuck that had left her unsatisfied and craving something...more. There'd been no real feeling, no real connection. Dane might be little more than a stranger, but they shared something far stronger and far deeper than anything she'd ever experienced before. He brought her to life.

"Sweetheart, are you okay?"

She nodded and then realized his face was swimming above hers with her vision blurred. She swiped at a tear escaping down her face. "I've never been better," she whispered.

He gave her a look that was incredibly tender and said hoarsely, "You and me both."

She swallowed back the lump in her throat. She was stronger now! "There's only one thing that would make me even happier." At his nod, "I want to be on top." She couldn't lose control, not yet. To be in charge was something to be relished, revered even. Caleb hadn't just dictated in the boardroom, he had in the bedroom too.

With a wolfish smile that said he wouldn't mind a bit, Dane flipped her effortlessly around, changing their positions so that she straddled him. She leaned down with a smile and a queer ache behind her breasts. She wanted more than one more time with Dane. But it was an impossible wish. This joining would be their first and their last.

His breath caught when she pressed a kiss to a white raised scar near his collarbone. She straightened, exhaling with a rush as his hands moved to cup her breasts, his thumb and forefingers rolling her nipples until she let her head fall back, sighing with delight.

He was still stroking and caressing her breasts when, taking hold of the length of his cock, she tilted her hips and aligned him to the wet, opened slit of her cunt. She paused, anticipating the sensation, and Dane growled—a growl that morphed into a groan as she pushed down and impaled herself on his shaft, her muscles sheathing him tight.

"Oh, Dane," she breathed. His large cock so deep inside felt so damn good, so damn right! Dane's moan morphed into a low growl as she started to rock, setting a rhythm as old as time while she memorized the feel of him deep within, drawing out the moment until she couldn't help but move faster and faster, gasping at the ever-increasing sensation building within.

Until a sob tore from her throat and she was tumbling straight into an abyss of exquisite pleasure, Dane plummeting right along with her.

Chapter Six

Late afternoon sunlight streamed through the slats of the window when she abruptly woke. She sat bolt upright, ears straining, pulses thundering as she searched her surroundings, before she subsided back into Dane's arms with the realization of where she was, who she was with.

Dane lay watching her with drowsy contemplation. "Hi, sleepyhead," he murmured.

"Hi," she managed, suddenly shy.

He cupped a hand behind her head and tugged her in close for a kiss. "Thank you." At her obviously bemused look, he added, "For trusting me."

"You're welcome." She snuggled further into his arms, content to stay put. At least for now. "I only wish I could stay like this forever," she conceded.

He stroked her head. "And why can't you?"

She twisted in his embrace and looked into his face, feeling all too serious. "That little secret I said I had—"

"Ah." His jaw hardened fractionally. "Go on."

"It was my fiancé. Was. He's my ex-fiancé now." She lifted a hand, letting it drop back to her side as she added, "Only, try telling him that. He's...he's a very possessive man."

Dane's face remained impassive. He reached for her hand, interlacing her fingers with his and examining her bare ring finger.

"I left my engagement ring behind on my pillow." She chewed her lower lip. "It belongs in my past, not my future."

The ring had represented a future bound by sacred vows to love, cherish and uphold. Everything her relationship with Caleb wasn't. The only vow she felt certain Caleb would have kept was the death do us part.

Looking back, it was so hard to believe that Caleb had been such a rock for her after the death of her parents in a car accident. She'd just turned twenty, and though on the outside she'd put on a brave face, inside her world had spun off its axis. She'd been an only child, with no one to share her grief. Add the mountain of debt that had been left behind, and she'd been only too grateful to allow Caleb—a man her parents had known for years but seemed somehow to disapprove of—to take the reins.

Trouble was, he'd never handed those reins back to her. It hadn't taken her long to see his true colors, hadn't taken long to understand why her parents had felt such mistrust toward him. She'd lived in terror of him, too scared to leave him, too scared not to. But after the first time he'd hit her, she'd known there was no future with him, known she'd never marry him.

More than once her refusal to wed had sent Caleb right over the edge.

Dane drifted his thumb over her bare finger. "You had no choice but to leave," he murmured. "You were compelled to find me."

"I'm not sure I understand," she said softly.

"You don't have to understand." He turned to her fully, pressing soft kisses onto her brow, the tip of her nose, before finally claiming her mouth until she all but melted into his heat. He drew back to add huskily, "Just follow your instincts, trust in them."

He moved his body full-length over hers, his weight centered on his forearms and his outspread hands on either side of her head. "Now shut up and kiss me," he said huskily.

She smiled as intoxicated delight sizzled through her womb and spread outward, her mouth capturing the soft heat of his lips this time until she became lost in everything but the moment. Dane broke the kiss first. Then he was leaning back between her legs to sit on his heels. His hungry stare devoured her nakedness, sending skittish goose bumps all over her body, her nipples tightening harder still, jutting like edible beacons. "I want to taste your pussy," he all but growled.

At any other time, with anyone else, such a request would have had her deliver an emphatic and outraged *no*. Caleb hadn't called her frigid for nothing. She'd never enjoyed sex with him, and though she'd eventually acted the part of his sex slave with award-winning passion, he'd known it for the lie it was.

She nodded assent, a little scared but burning hot for him too.

Dane's large hands encircled her thighs and tugged her down toward him. He spread her legs wider still, exposing her wet pussy to his gaze. "Exquisite," he said on a sigh. Then he lifted her high and his head dipped.

She let out a strangled moan when his tongue lapped at her flesh, wet strokes that were just hard and fast enough to build pleasure, to tease and tantalize. His mouth moved like a heat-seeking missile, suckling on her swollen clit until the act verged on pleasure-pain, and she teetered right on the cusp of a climax.

He drew back, a knowing smile curling his pussy-moist lips. "Not yet," he said huskily, pulling her closer still and planting her legs around his hips. "Not quite yet." He rotated his hips, the head of his oozing cock teasing her cunt lips and the quivering flesh around her channel.

She whimpered. She wanted his big cock inside her. "Take me now...please!"

His smile crooking into a triumphant grin, he drove his cock deep inside. She cried out ecstasy, amazed by their oneness, the perfect fit. The way the friction of his cock instantly ignited her cunt back to life. He withdrew, and at her mewl of distress, he thrust back inside, taking up with an ever-increasing rhythm that left her dizzy with swift, escalating rapture.

Her head fell back and she let out a startled moan, coming with fierce, convulsive shudders that milked his cock as he too climaxed with a long drawn-out sigh, his hot seed exploding inside her.

They were both breathing heavily when Dane gently withdrew. He lay alongside her, and she turned to face him, her heart squeezing to see the same awed gratification in his stare that no doubt shone in her own.

He leaned forward, their long kiss a drowsy after-play that somehow twisted her insides sharper than their lovemaking. She had to leave. And soon. She pulled away and sat up, drawing her knees to her chest and tunneling a hand over her face. "I should go," she whispered, yearning to stay.

The mattress moved as Dane sat up beside her. He brushed some hair from her brow, and it was nice this once not to flinch, nice this once to marvel at the honey warmth unfurling inside her.

"Don't you see?" He cupped her chin and turned her head toward him. He searched her face, seeking answers she was too afraid to give. "You might be running from your ex, but you were searching for me."

Hope spiraled before fear spiked her from the inside out, deflating her. She pulled free but stayed facing him as she rested her cheek on one of her knees. "Even if you're right, I can't stay."

His eyes narrowed. "You fear your ex?"

Yes. She shrugged, going for casual but failing miserably. "You don't know what Caleb is capable of."

He shifted forward, his attention wholly focused on her. "Caleb?" The breath left his lungs in a savage, disbelieving hiss. "Caleb Marsden?"

She frowned. "Yes. You know him?"

He nodded, his expression becoming hard, glacial. "Damn it to hell, I should have guessed!" He released a heavy breath. "I think it's time we had that talk."

She felt dizzy suddenly, weak. "I'm not sure I'm ready to—" Something thudded downstairs, a rather inconsequential noise, yet they were both instantly alert.

Dane held up a hand, signaling for her to stay where she was, to stay quiet. She nodded, remaining motionless while her ears strained for further sound, her pulse racing and trepidation filling her veins.

He moved off the bed and toward the walk-in closet with feline stealth, the muscles in his back and shoulders bunched, his buttocks taut. Carefully opening the sliding door, he grabbed the nearest shirt and tossed it to her.

It took less than a minute to thrust her arms into its long white sleeves and button the front. Dane took half that time to step into a pair of jeans and zipper them up. In his fluid, silent tread, he returned to her. His nostrils flaring, he said quietly, "Caleb has come to claim you."

She closed her eyes. She didn't know how Dane knew this for sure, but she perceived all too well what he said was true. Her worst fears had come to haunt her. Only, this time she wasn't alone. Lids flicking open, she shook her head and whispered, "I'm not going anywhere with him. I'm not his, I never have been." Her hands fisted at her sides. "I'll wait here until you get back."

Dane leaned over and pressed a swift, hard kiss to her mouth. His eyes glittered. "I love you." Then moving swiftly to the door, opening and then shutting it with a click behind him, he was gone.

She pressed shaky fingertips to her mouth. Terror and apprehension were all but forgotten, a whole gamut of emotions washing over her in an exquisite starburst of color. *I love you too.* She never thought she'd love again...not so soon and not this deeply.

A sob crept up in her throat. Had she left it too late to tell him? Was Caleb going to rob her of someone else she loved? She lifted her chin. She was done with hiding. Done with cowering. She was done with Caleb. Period.

It was past time to make a stand. She'd fight for her freedom. She'd fight for Dane.

Gunshot ricocheted through the house, a single, booming crack of noise. For a millisecond she stayed put, inwardly reeling with utter, soul-destroying shock. "No!"

She scrambled off the bed and sprinted for the door. Jerking it open, she raced along the hallway and down the stairs, ignoring her own danger. She no longer cared what her violent ex would do to her. She cared only what he'd do to Dane.

She skidded to a stop. Nausea burned like acid in her belly, searing her throat.

"Hello, sweetheart." Caleb lounged at the foot of the stairs, his spiked blond hair highlighting the crooked, cruel smile that detracted every bit of handsomeness from his face. But it was the vision of a semiconscious Dane crumpled beside Caleb, his head and torso inert on the floor, his legs twisted behind him and propped on the lower steps, which stopped her breath, her heart.

Dane, no! Horror filled her, leaving her cold and sick inside. Little wonder she'd woken earlier feeling uneasy. Her instincts had been trying to warn her—if only she'd listened. Her eyes burning, she cast a hateful look at Caleb. "What have you done?"

Caleb smirked. A pearl-gray Armani suit emphasized the manic glitter in his eyes and matched the Magnum rifle held loosely in one of his hands. "What does it look like, slut?"

Nothing Caleb said could hurt her anymore, she was well and truly immune to his taunts now. But she immediately sensed Dane's bristling anger as he struggled to move. He dragged himself forward. His feet plopped down first one step, and then the other, dark blood smearing the floor behind him.

Her chest swelled at his courage, his love, even as anxiety flared. She had to get him to a hospital. "Dane—"

"Go near him," Caleb said softly but with utter certainty, "and you're both dead."

Staring down the barrel of Caleb's firearm, she knew he meant every word. Dane raised his head, blood oozing from a graze on his brow. Focusing on Caleb, he grated, "Leave Elyse out of it. This is between you and me."

Caleb laughed, the mirthless sound chilling. "On the contrary. Elyse is the only thing between me and you, my old friend."

Old friend?

A pain stabbed her right in the heart. Her attention all on Dane, she asked, "Caleb knows you?" Then, her eyes widening, she breathed, "You're *the* Dane Maddox." The one and same man Caleb hated with a passion. And though it seemed too impossible to contemplate—Dane should be a crotchety old man, not a virile male in his prime who was, at most, a decade older than she—somehow she knew it was true.

Caleb's delighted laugh chilled the air as he swung the firearm between them with the ease of an expert gunman. "Dane hasn't told you anything, has he?"

Nausea twisted her gut even harder, but she refused to give Caleb an answer. All her focus centered on the man she'd fallen in love with, a man she knew next to nothing about. Terrible thoughts leaked into her mind like poison. Dane had everything Caleb didn't—except her.

She backed up a step. Did Dane truly love her, or was she just a trophy to be won in the battle between two rivals?

"Elyse." Dane breathed heavily, his eyes somehow intense even as he suffered through what had to be agonizing pain. "Trust in me. Trust in the moonlight. It's all I ask."

Tears welled as she all but drowned in the tender warmth of his stare. Though it all made too much sense now and she should distrust him, somehow she couldn't doubt him. His life was in danger, and all he was concerned about was her faith, her belief in him.

How had she ever thought him cold?

Caleb moved suddenly, climbing the few steps toward her. She had no time to do anything but hiss out a breath of pain when he grabbed a fistful of her hair and hauled her close. "Let's do this the easy way, hmm?" he said, his voice menacing and low.

Elyse knew better than to fight, at least, not with her body—her mind, he would never tame. Resisting only gave Caleb more reason to inflict pain. But it was immediately apparent it's what he intended anyway as he jerked her even harder against him, slamming the back of her head to his iron chest.

Training the rifle on Dane, he flung his other arm across her throat, blocking off her windpipe. She fought then, desperately, frantically, even as she felt her energy falter, the room start to spin.

It was then Dane came to life. Springing from the floor, he let out an inhuman growl, his eyes glowing, shimmering. With a knowing chuckle, Caleb loosened his stranglehold and tugged her with him a few steps higher. He motioned toward Dane and said coldly, "See for yourself, my faithless fiancée—"

I'm not your fiancée.

"See what your lover has been hiding." She gasped in clean, welcome draughts of air. Her very life was at threat, yet her mind whirred at the implications right in front of her eyes.

Dane...wasn't Dane.

Clasping her borrowed shirt together at the front, she watched in stunned horror as Dane's face broadened. Bones snapped and his jaw grew, his throat thickening and the slipknot on the leather cord at his neck giving way. His eyes rolled back as his face formed into something too large to be a...dog? His arms became forelegs, his legs hind legs. Black fur pushed through his skin and made him resemble some huge wolf.

A fierce, primal beast.

Chapter Seven

"That's impossible," she whispered. Yet suddenly she knew it wasn't. Not just because she was seeing it with her own eyes. Her heart already knew what her mind recollected.

Crystal-clear memories rushed back one after the other, making her only too aware why this creature was so familiar. She'd met Dane in his werewolf form just outside the cabin, when she'd been in her werewolf form. She remembered everything! But mostly, she remembered how smitten with lust she'd been and how right and powerful their attraction had been.

"Yes, impossible for the rest of us werewolves," Caleb agreed harshly, pulling her from her thoughts.

"Werewolves," she breathed. Somehow saying the word aloud made it all seem so much more difficult to contemplate. More real.

"Yes. Dane can change at will." His lip curled. "Whereas we...we have to wait until the rise of each full moon."

"We?" Her voice cracked. Caleb waved his firearm toward Dane. "Lover boy told you nothing, did he?" Caleb said scornfully. "I'm a werewolf just like you."

She guessed anyone else would have been sickened, disgusted, horrified and appalled at the thought of being a lycan, just like the violent, cruel man before her. Somehow she wasn't.

She'd never been unfeeling like Caleb. And She'd always felt different, an outsider. Even as Caleb's rich fiancée perhaps more so—she'd felt poles apart from their peers. An outcast. But now it all seemed so clear. Her dreams, her sleepwalking, it all fell together like the final pieces of a difficult puzzle.

Little wonder she had nothing in common with their human friends. She shuddered. Except for her genus, she had even less in common to her lycan ex-lover. Dane was the one and only person she felt anchored to, connected with.

"What, nothing to say?" Caleb jeered. Looking her up and down, he added, "You might have the looks, but you always were a mouse at heart."

She didn't look away, didn't back down. "And you always were second best." Suddenly she cared less if she was hurt. Dane had given her strength, given her something to fight for. "It must be hard to live in Dane's shadow."

Caleb snared her again, quicker than a snake strike, his forearm locking around her throat with brutal force. Even as she was choking, his warm breath feathered her ear when he said, "You forget, I've got the one, the only thing he wants."

Dane lunged up the stairs then, snarling and snapping, the black ruff along his neck and back bristling, his long canines glinting in the dying rays of sunlight streaming through the windows around them. Elyse had no doubt Dane could hear and understand their every word.

"Steady, Fido," Caleb rasped. "You're wasting what little strength you have." When he jammed the barrel of the gun against the side of Elyse's temple, she couldn't hold back a strangled sob. Caleb clicked off the safety and added, "And she'll die for nothing."

With a growl of challenge, Dane leapt. Caleb swung the rifle his way and fired. The werewolf yelped, then dropped into a bloodied heap at the stairs by their feet. Elyse screamed, but it was all on the inside. She was a shell to the million emotions tangled within, scrambling for a foothold on a reality she couldn't accept.

Caleb descended the steps, pulling her stiff and numb form beside him. He turned back, throwing one last scornful look at the werewolf. "You let your heart rule your head, my friend."

Caleb abruptly released her. But she couldn't move, couldn't make a sound as, like a mirage flickering back into reality, she watched the unconscious beast turn human. Dane's face was ashen, lifeless. Blood poured from his chest wound, dribbling down each step before puddling onto the floor.

A deep, unrelenting ache filled a void behind her breasts. When she turned to Caleb, she felt all the hatred, her loathing, burn in her stare. "What have you done?"

"Don't worry," Caleb jeered. "Your lover isn't dead...not yet. The silver bullet may have forced him to turn human while unconscious, but he'll live. I have much worse in store for him yet."

He pushed at Dane's leg with the toe of his shiny boot and watched with palpable satisfaction as the limb flopped back. "Even in human form a silver bullet will only knock him out for a few hours at best."

The ache spread until she was once again numb all over, the fiery hatred doused within and leaving her cold. Unfeeling. She didn't...couldn't fight Caleb as he dragged her outside to his waiting car.

Two men in black suits stood at the ready on either side of the sedan, the machine guns in their hands seemingly extensions of themselves. Caleb motioned with a nod for the bodyguards to get into the front. He pushed Elyse into the backseat and slid in beside her. "Go," he commanded the driver.

She refused to look behind her, refused to let even one sob escape her tight lips. She refused to give Caleb the satisfaction.

"Well now, sweetheart." His lip curled at the word. "I'm going to enjoy taming you back into submission."

She stared straight ahead, keeping the sudden, deep shudder all on the inside as he curled a finger around a lock of her hair and said, "It is, after all, what we alpha males do."

Elyse turned away, and though her hair pulled tight in Caleb's grip, making her scalp tingle and burn, she stared unflinchingly out the window. He let her go with a hard chuckle, but she concentrated instead on the sky with its growing sweep of darkening indigo, the faraway horizon in the throes of a spectacular red-orange sunset. The tips of the eucalyptus trees were bathed in gold light, the rocky terrain darker shades of red.

Blood red. She swallowed hard. She couldn't think about Dane, couldn't dwell on her feelings, her shame. He would live, and for now, that would have to be enough. She would find a way to return to Dane. She'd find a way for them to be together, or die trying.

Chapter Eight

The leather seat creaked as Caleb leaned forward and said, "Hurry it up, boys. It will be dark soon."

She turned to him and croaked, "Where are you taking me?"

Caleb leaned back with a smirk, flinging out an arm and curling it around her shoulders before pulling her suffocatingly close. "Somewhere near. You can call it the honeymoon we never had."

She stiffened. "No matter where you take me, you can't force me to stay. I'll always find a way to leave."

Caleb threw his head back and laughed, but there was even less warmth to his obvious amusement than before. "See, that's where you're wrong, dearest," he said scathingly. He forced her chin up, forcing her gaze to meet his. "You won't be going anywhere."

There was such assurance in his voice, such triumph in his stare, she couldn't help but half believe him, couldn't help but ask, "What makes you say that?"

"It's simple, really." One of his fair eyebrows lifted condescendingly. "After tonight, you'll be compelled to stay."

He was telling the truth. She'd lived with Caleb long enough to know when he meant every word. And he most assuredly did now.

"The full moon of your twenty-fifth year is the deciding factor. Once we're joined, your werewolf instincts will see us bonded. Permanently." He smirked. "There will be no worse torment than two destined lycans kept apart, despite themselves."

"You're insane," she whispered.

Sick. Twisted.

His grin dropped and his face darkened. Then he nodded, simmering violence abated. For now. "Perhaps." He shrugged. "But you'll soon discover one has to be a little crazy to live the way we do."

When the car turned into a pebbled driveway, which cut into an endless sea of eucalyptus trees, he released her and leaned forward again.

He peered through the windshield, his body language all but singing with anticipation. "At last. We're here."

She closed her eyes, resting her brow on the passenger's tinted window. Her belly churned at what she would face ahead, the sickness within abating only as Dane's words echoed in her mind.

Believe in yourself. Believe in the moonlight.

The words triggered immediate empowerment. As a werewolf she hadn't just been physically transformed, she had emotionally and mentally too. No longer had she been a helpless, demoralized human. She'd been powerful, mighty and formidable.

She opened her eyes and raised her chin. She would never forget that feeling, never allow that part of herself—human or beast—to slip through the cracks until she was just a shadow of her true self. Deep inside she would always be a werewolf. She always had been.

The car drew to a stop at a set of huge iron gates. The driver leaned out the window and keyed a code into a numerical pad set into a post before the gates slid apart in barely a whisper of sound.

Elyse noted the security cameras affixed to the top of stone pillars as they drove through, and realized there would be no easy escape. This place had been set up like a fortress.

A huge four-story ochre-rendered house sat on top of a gently sloping hill some hundred or so meters away, surrounded by tall, shaggy palm trees.

"What is this place?" she croaked.

She heard Caleb's sigh of satisfaction as he informed, "I bought this land, built this house, the very moment I discovered Dane had chosen to stay close by, in wait for his lifemate."

So her European friends she'd hitched a ride with were safe. That was something, at least.

She swung back to him, and he clucked his tongue and added, "With so few of us lycans in the world, and you clearly not my intended, there was a good chance you would be drawn to him." His expression grew fierce, ugly. "Drawn to the oldest and apparently most powerful alpha male."

"You asked me to marry you, knowing all this?" she asked, disbelieving.

His blue eyes cut like ice. "Dane has everything else. He wasn't having you too."

So he'd never loved her after all.

She'd known that, of course she had. But to have it announced with such cold clarity was like a sucker punch to the gut.

The car stopped at the end of a horseshoe driveway. After the men in the front seat climbed out, Caleb indicated she get out too.

She did so slowly, reluctantly.

A woman with shoulder-length dark hair pushed through the double doors of the large house. Giving Elyse a look of burning hatred, she bestowed Caleb a stiff nod and then slid into the driver's seat of the car. With the wheels kicking up stones, the woman sent the car roaring back in the direction they'd come from.

Caleb was taking away all means of escape, she realized numbly. He wasn't taking any chances.

The minders stood a discreet distance away as their boss faced Elyse. Stooping into a half bow and sweeping out a hand that was pure mockery, he informed, "Welcome to your new home."

"You mean my prison?" Nodding to his men, she added, "Along with my guards."

He caught her arm and jerked her into step beside him. Striding toward the entrance doors, he drawled, "Very observant. So tell me, what am I in this picture you paint?"

She released a hoarse laugh. "My worst nightmare."

His fingers dug into her arm when he forced her to a stop. He jerked her around to face him. "You'll pay for that," he said softly. He raised a hand, and she flinched involuntarily. He smiled, the back of his hand trailing like the touch of a feather down her cheek as he added, "You'll pay for that big-time."

There was something far more dangerous in that gentle touch than what he usually delivered. Her belly lurched even as she told herself he no longer terrified her. He was simmering violence waiting to erupt. "I've paid more than enough already," she said.

From her peripheral she saw the bodyguards exchange a look, clearly awkward yet fascinated by Caleb and his ex-lover's dispute. "I paid from the moment I trusted you. From the first time you hit me." His face darkened, but she was beyond caring now. She heaved in a breath and finished tightly, "But mostly I paid from the moment you killed our unborn child."

She didn't feel any pain when he clouted her across the face. She was only aware of the great crack of sound when his fist smashed into her jaw, of flying backward and falling hard. It was almost involuntary to snap her thighs together, ensuring he never saw or touched her there again.

Only Dane had that right now.

Something warm trickled down her chin, her throat. She lifted an unsteady hand and swiped at the wetness, her hand coming away red and sticky. She looked up, seeing double as Caleb slowly shook his head. "I never meant to hurt you, my dear, but sometimes you do ask for it." He stepped closer. "I never wanted our love to cause you pain."

She shook her head. "You're mistaken. I feel nothing but pity for you."

His eyes narrowed, then hardened into cruel slits. "Oh? Is it pity you feel when I tell you I arranged a mechanic to sabotage your parents' car, killing them?"

Her heart stopped. Everything slowed. "No." She shook her head. "No!"

"Yes." He smirked. "I couldn't have their dislike stand in the way of our budding relationship, now, could I?"

She repressed the deep shudders inside, repressed everything as she breathed, "Don't you understand? It's all been for nothing. I don't love you. I never have. Dane is the only man I'll ever love."

When he stalked toward her, his face black with rage, she knew his next punch wouldn't be restrained. This time when he hit her she saw nothing but sudden darkness.

Chapter Nine

Dane woke in varying degrees of awareness, but with just one thing on his mind.

Elyse.

Caleb had her now, and Dane could only imagine what the man...lowlife, would do to her. He gritted his teeth, willing his body to move. He had to get to her before Caleb coupled with her in their human form at the peak of the full moon.

A vein throbbed to life at his temple, rage leaving him gasping and dizzy. But still he couldn't move, not for some minutes, not with his blood fighting off the effects of the damn silver bullet. It was only lucky his immortal body recognized and was able to eject any foreign matter from its point of entry.

The silver bullets were further evidence just how low and dishonorable Caleb had become. It was forbidden for a lycan to use such a weapon on another lycan. Not only was their species on the knife edge of extinction, it was pack law for two warring alphas to fight one-on-one, using canines, strength and cunning.

He groaned, hurting all over. But at last he was able to roll over and sit on the edge of the steps, groggily trying to get his bearings like he imagined a drunk would on an all-night bender.

He looked down, brushing ineffectually at the sticky, half-congealed blood covering his torso and thighs. His chest ached. His heart. "Bloody hell."

He should have told Elyse the truth from the very start. He should have told her what she was...what he was. He should have, but he hadn't. Instead, her ex-fiancé had delivered the news before forcing her to leave.

He staggered to his feet, breathing heavily and resisting the sudden urge to empty the contents of his belly. He looked out the window. The light was fading fast. Thank god. The moon would be out soon. It would facilitate his healing. But like a double-edged sword, it would also bring on Elyse's change—and Caleb's obvious plan to mate with her and make her his.

Permanently.

Over my dead and rotting body.

A short time later he was in an icy-cold shower that brought him back to life like a slap to the face. Outspread hands pushed against the tiles on either side, he hung his head, giving himself just one minute as he watched the water wash the blood down the drain in a frothy pink swirl. It took perhaps another five minutes to dress and then descend the stairs, elated to feel the slow but gradual return of his strength.

With the rise of the full moon, he'd be almost totally re-energized. He stepped outside. "Son of a bitch!" He circled his SUV with growing anger. Every tire had been slashed, the vehicle sitting on its rims. It wouldn't be going anywhere.

He didn't bother wasting further precious energy and time undressing to make the change to werewolf. Sprinting to the edge of an embankment, he leapt through the air.

His clothes wrenched apart well before he landed on all four paws, where he half-skated, half-ran down the last of the incline, using his tail like a rudder. Caleb may have slowed him down, but he'd overlooked a critical factor. Dane knew this land like the back of his hand. He knew every shortcut, every landmark. And he'd been working on his endurance, honing his speed.

Already swift, he could travel faster and farther than he ever had before. Elyse's welfare spurred him on like nothing else could. He'd mated with her, bonded with her. And now his internal radar—more instinctive perception than anything else—would allow him to follow her to the ends of the earth, if need be.

Yes, Caleb would be expecting him…just not so soon. Elyse and Caleb would get to know each other as werewolves before they changed back to mortal to satisfy their primal urges. He had a little time…he hoped.

Dane was breathing hard by the time he came to a driveway that cut like a river through the trees. He wasn't yet at full strength, despite the round moon clearing the horizon like a big fat jewel. His fast, loping run that ate up the ground had also eaten up much of his energy. He would have to rely almost solely on his cunning and foresight.

Chapter Ten

Elyse awoke to darkness broken by shafts of moonlight streaming through the wall-to-ceiling glass windows, and to the pain of werewolf change barreling through her body.

Don't fight it. The more you do, the worse it gets.

Dane's advice replayed in her head like a mantra, over and over, and she was only vaguely aware of her cry that evolved into a howl as she gave herself up to the inevitable. Feeling like she was having an out-of-body experience, Elyse was distantly aware of the ferociousness of the change, of her bones breaking and expanding, her borrowed shirt tearing and falling apart, her fur emerging and tufting into a coat, her tail forming.

But she knew surrendering to the change had brought it on strong and swift, the pain almost immediately forgotten. Instead, she was consumed by a desire that zinged through her veins, heating her from the inside out.

Need, undiluted and hot, left her panting and restless. Caleb in his unfamiliar male lycan form, padded toward her. She whined uncertainty as a desperate, wanton yearning filled her, despite her hatred toward this white-furred beast...to Caleb in any form.

She lifted her snout and breathed in his testosterone scent, disturbed by the surging primal instincts that reviled this lycan, even as it was enticed almost beyond endurance. She whined again and he moved forward, prancing.

They touched noses and she saw the flare of lust in his blue eyes, a lust reciprocated with her loins twisting in response. Her ears flickered as he growled dominance, baring his teeth. She snarled back, nipping at the ruff under his throat. And suddenly their passion was tempered with the need to dominate, to control, to bring the other beast to heel.

The male lycan used his brute strength and weight to knock her off her feet. She was down but quickly on her feet and darting away, out of range of his snapping canines. Bounding past, she bit into his soft flank, past his thick coat to tear into flesh and draw blood, warm and metallic.

He whipped around, snarling and forcing her onto her side beneath him. This isn't how it's meant to be, she thought distantly. Her encounter with Dane in their lycan form had been like a meeting of souls, a knowing acceptance, an amorous but tender greeting.

She struggled harder for leverage, snapping at the fierce male pinning her down with uncompromising brute force. In his usual style, he went straight for her throat, his huge jaw locking over her windpipe until she felt herself go limp, unconsciousness beckoning yet again.

It was an unwilling surrender, and Caleb snarled warning the moment he released hold, his icy stare flashing as she gasped in great lungfuls of oxygen. Ceding to his will seemed to trigger a reverse change, one she fought against with all her might.

But excruciating stabs of pain racked her body even before her bones began to snap and shrink, her fur withdrawing as her tail retracted. She saw that Caleb too was going through the change back to mortal. And then, as much as she fought it, she felt herself sliding into a blissful void of nothingness.

Elyse woke in her human body, to the sound of loud automatic gunfire somewhere outside. She heard a scream, running footsteps, another scream. Then intense silence. Somehow she couldn't find the will to care. Not when her every cell ached with a need that set her whole body aflame. She wanted to be touched, kissed...taken.

Nothing else mattered. She wanted sex with the single-minded desperation of an addict. "Dane," she whispered.

The hand curling like a vise around her bare shoulder wasn't the touch she craved. Her skin crawled, but withholding a shudder, she turned to Caleb. "Not this time." He smiled, but there was no warmth in his face, only cold-hearted desire and leering triumph. "This time, you'll be all mine. And this time, you'll want me despite yourself."

Revulsion trickled down her spine, killing all the hunger she'd experienced in werewolf form as she viewed his nakedness. His pale chest gleamed in the moonlight, his balls heavy beneath his cock that rose like a mottled purple snake about to strike.

Caleb really assumed she still wanted him. Yet somehow, against everything he believed, everything perhaps the lycans believed, she didn't. Not one bit. There was only one man...one werewolf for her. And he was close by. She sensed him with every atom of her being.

Her heart surged, her blood singing through her veins. Dane was coming for her. "Come here," Caleb ordered thickly. He seemed oblivious to anything but his own needs, to anything but their joining.

She looked up at him with what she hoped was a seductive smile. It wouldn't be the first time she'd pretended to want him. Too many times she'd endured Caleb's groping, his hot breath on her face, his tongue pushing into her mouth, gagging her. At first she'd tried to be immune, to distance herself—until her lack of response had seen her pummeled into obedience.

In the end she'd acted the role of his perfect lover, the model trophy wife-to-be living in constant fear of reprisal. This night would be her best performance, and her last. She would never be subjected to Caleb's self-absorbed, cruel needs again.

She held out a hand, her belly heaving as he took hold and jerked her upright, slamming her against him so that his arousal jutted against her belly. She swallowed past the bile searing her throat. "No more fooling around," he growled.

With his hands clamping her ass cheeks, she blanked out the too-familiar feel of his soft, smooth touch. Standing on tiptoe, she said into his ear, "I'm sorry." His eyes flashed uncertainty, momentarily dulling lust. "What?"

Moving forward to unbalance him, she brought her other knee up, crunching hard between his legs, his bloated balls. He dropped to the floor with a strangled grunt of pain. "I'm sorry you ever mistook me for a mouse at heart."

She spun away and headed toward the door. Turning the handle and yanking on it, she realized it was locked from the inside, the key removed. "Shit." Her pulses jumping with anxiety, she pulled harder, rattling the door that appeared to be solid, reinforced wood.

Caleb wouldn't be down and hurting for long.

She heard footsteps approaching from the other side of the door, sensed immediately it was Dane even before her hand dropped away from the doorknob. "Dane, I'm here. I can't get out. The door is locked."

She heard his savage expletive, and then he said hoarsely, reassuringly, "I'll get you out."

Of course he would.

She heard Caleb chuckle behind her, the sound coarse, grating. When she spun around, he was still sprawled out on the floor, his face contorted like a madman's. "Looking for this?" Caleb asked, a crooked smirk marring his model-handsome face as he reached across the floor to what was left of his shredded pants and pulled out a large key from a pocket.

"It's over, Caleb," she said. "It was over even before I left my engagement ring on our bed."

His eyes radiated feral hatred. "It isn't over until I say it is."

"Elyse!" Dane hammered on the solid wooden door and then used all his weight to pound against it. It was only then Elyse realized no one could save her—not even Dane. No one could help her, except her. And for once, fear was no longer her common ground.

She lifted her chin, holding Caleb's vicious stare. "It's over because I say it's over." She stepped toward him. His eyes widened and then narrowed like a cobra's. But she was beyond caring. From the moment she'd known she was lycan, she'd changed mentally as much as physically.

He clambered to his feet and met her halfway, his fists bunched. "Seems to me it's past time to remind you who is boss."

Anger surged, taken over swiftly by a shaft of power that zapped through her veins like a thunderclap. When he raised a fist and let it swing, she caught his fist in her hand—her paw—the size of a saucer. Adrenaline buzzed. She could change parts of her body at will!

"That's impossible," he said through gritted teeth. "No lycan can partly morph. And the full moon wields no power now it's past its peak and you've succumbed to sexual thrall."

"Who said anything about succumbing?" she asked. Then giving him a shove, she propelled him yards away into a wall. As he slumped to the floor she stepped toward him and leaned down. Plucking the key from his fist with her one human hand, she said, "It seems I've broken a lot of werewolf codes today."

The door splintered behind her, then burst off its hinges with Dane's next hard kick. She dropped the key onto the floor with a clatter, and with an offhand shrug mused, "Seems I don't need the key, after all."

Chapter Eleven

Dane strode toward her and pulled her into his arms. His mouth covered hers in a brief, hard kiss that spoke volumes before he pulled back and asked huskily, "Are you all right?"

She nodded, hiccupping at the sudden eruption of emotions threatening to overcome her. She pulled back from him and lifted her one shifted paw. "I think so."

He whistled, a sound of awe. "You have the gift to change at will. I'd suspected as much when you had all the signs of changing at the cabin in daylight." Cupping her face, he kissed her again, pulling back to search her eyes and concede, "You really are someone special. Someone precious."

She glowed inside. "You know what? I think I'm starting to believe you." It seemed with her belief came instant control. She grimaced as her blood hummed, the bones in her paw snapping, shifting.

She looked up at Dane with a smile. Only, he was frowning down at her now, his fingers gently brushing beneath the still-sensitive skin of her eye.

"Caleb did this?" he asked.

She nodded. "At least the burn on my leg is all healed now," she said, trying to ease the sudden tension emanating from him. Seeing his tender expression become hard, fierce, ruthless, she could easily imagine him as the Dane Maddox, businessman extraordinaire. Behind his human persona, his eyes glinted with a malice that was all primitive werewolf.

Caleb, too, clearly perceived Dane's intention and struggled onto his feet. Dane's focus swung to the other man. The next instant, he flew at Caleb, pinning him back against the wall, his hands wrapped around his throat. Caleb's eyes bulged as Dane said, "You dare touch my *weren*, go near her again, and you have my lycan word I'll come looking for you." He leaned close. "And we will fight to the death."

Dane loosened his hold and Caleb's head lolled forward. A coward to the end. "She's all yours," Caleb muttered.

Dane dropped the other man with a grunt of disgust. "I no longer acknowledge you as a rival alpha male. I no longer acknowledge you as a lycan." Caleb didn't try to dispute him, and unbelievably Elyse felt a momentary twinge of pity for him.

Dane moved back to her and drew her near, his arm around her shoulders. And just then Elyse realized she had never felt safer or more protected. "I'm taking you home with me," Dane murmured huskily. "Where you belong. If that is what you want."

"More than anything," she said simply. Walking with him through the shattered door and down the stairs, she felt as if she were living an incredible dream and any minute she would wake up.

For too long she'd lived a nightmare, but now the future beckoned to her with the brilliance of a beacon.

A clatter of high heels coming up the stairs had her focus drawn to the woman whom she'd seen earlier, driving off in Caleb's car. In knee-high boots, a white pants suit and her green eyes flashing fire, the female was cat woman personified.

Caleb might well be dominated by this woman, just as he had dominated Elyse. She couldn't help but secretly smile. Karma would win out.

Seemingly oblivious to their naked state, the woman flicked back a lock of her dark hair before all but purring, "Where is Caleb? What have you done to him?"

Elyse exchanged a conspiratorial look with Dane before jerking her head in the upstairs vicinity. "He's all yours."

As Elyse and Dane walked outside, heavy rain suddenly broke free from the clouds, splattering the dry gum leaves like castanets before falling like miniature grenades onto the dry ground and firing chalky dust into the air.

When it rains I'll be coming back.

She turned to Dane, slipping her arms up over the wet, warm skin of his broad shoulders as she lifted her face to the sky. She closed her eyes for a moment, relishing in the icy rivulets pouring over her brow, down her cheeks, nose and chin, before dripping between her breasts, down her belly and thighs.

And in that moment, with the deluge falling from the sky, with no more to fear and the weight of her past lifted, she wanted nothing more than to celebrate life. To run...to fuck. In that order.

She looked up at him, a wide grin splitting her face. "Catch me if you can!"

She twisted away and bolted, willing werewolf change with a newfound conviction that flowed through her bloodstream like healing antibodies. The beast responded, roaring with a desire to break free, to break out. And it did. With brutal, unrelenting force.

She staggered, wrapping her arms around her torso before continuing on as fast as her body allowed. Though shifting to werewolf form hurt like hell, this time she was able to glory in the buzz of adrenaline that immediately followed, flooding her system like an illicit drug.

The heightened senses, the amazing strength and speed vibrated through her every cell, her every muscle, even before she dropped onto all fours. As beast, she stilled for a moment and cocked her ears backward, separating the sounds of the drumming downpour and picking up the crack and shift of bones as Dane began his own transformation.

He'd given her a good head start. Emitting a howl, she burst forward with phenomenal speed. The muddy ground suctioned at her paws, the dripping eucalyptus trees a blur as she headed southwest, aware precisely where she needed to go.

A huge red kangaroo burst into motion ahead, bounding in and out of the trees in full flight. Though these male marsupials were notoriously fast, she easily kept pace, giving into the chase and herding him in the direction she wanted to go—in the same way Dane had with her after her first change.

Her senses kicked into high alert seconds before she heard Dane closing in behind. The kangaroo slapped its tail onto the ground like a rudder, twisting and leaping one way with the honed instincts of a flight animal.

Exhilaration pulsed through Elyse's bloodstream as she lengthened her stride and surged straight ahead. Her lungs burned, her legs ached, her loins squeezing tight. Then Dane was beside her, his tongue lolling, his long, muscular legs easily eating up the ground.

The storm had passed, the rain settling into a soft patter when they burst through the trees, nose-to-nose, the cabin in their sights. She let loose another discordant yowl, feeding off the energy of the big black werewolf loping beside her, feeling alive and in wonderment of what—who she was.

Seeing the cabin was like coming home, and everything at last was right in her life.

A startlingly loud boom shattered her musings. Dane yelped, tumbling over and over before lying deathly still. She stopped, her beast mind for a moment not comprehending this new reality.

With a whine, she turned back, trotting over to Dane's unmoving form. The coppery scent of blood filled the air, overwhelming her werewolf senses. Another boom ricocheted through the valley, a ping that sprayed up dust and rocks right near her head.

A bullet!

A growl built up in her chest and tore from her throat. She nudged the werewolf with her nose, hearing his faint heartbeat even with the bloodied hole in his chest.

I don't want to leave you!

Only when her vision wavered in and out, the change coming upon her without her wanting it, did she have no choice but to lunge away, tearing out of sight among the trees. She couldn't let any human see her—not like this!

She gritted her teeth against the sudden spasms of remorseless pain. Her throat convulsed, her bones shuddering even as a pair of hunters, their rifles pointed in front of them, came into view from behind the cabin. Bastards! She went limp, aware fighting the pain would only prolong the shift. She needed to be human now. This once, unconsciousness didn't drag her under. She was stronger now, more able to endure the pain.

Within seconds she was pushing onto her bare feet, peering through the foliage and tree trunks. The hunters had stopped near Dane, leaning over him and gesturing with their hands, shaking their heads. They probably couldn't figure out what he was, what to do with him.

Wolves, especially one this huge, didn't belong in Australia. She crept forward, heart in her throat, picking up snatches of their conversation.

"I ain't never seen—"

"Too big for a wild dog."

One of the hunters prodded Dane with the barrel of his rifle, then clicking off the trigger's safety he raised the rifle to his level of sight.

"Hey!" She held back a petrified sob. She couldn't lose Dane, not now. Not ever! Damn it, she hadn't even told him she loved him.

She angled her chin and naked, stepped out from the cover of the trees. "What are you two doing with my dog?"

They looked up, their lust to kill turning too quickly into another type of lust as their eyes slid up and down her nudity.

"That don't look like any dog I've ever seen, pretty lady," the older of the two men said, rubbing his hand up and down the barrel of his gun.

The younger guy stepped toward her, licking his fleshy lower lip. "Looks to me like you'll be lonely now without your dog, and wanting a bit of company." He turned to the other man with a leering grin. "We sure don't mind obliging. We're housetrained and used to taking turns."

Dane stirred behind the two perverts facing her, and relief at his quick recovery warred with a nasty vileness from the other men. She had to act out this sick charade, prolong it for as long as she could. It shouldn't be too difficult. She'd had plenty of practice with Caleb.

She arched her back and slung outspread hands on her hips, pushing her breasts out. "You're too kind. I'm sure I wouldn't have known what to do with my time." She inwardly rolled her eyes. These men actually believed her innocent, sugar-sweet idiocy.

The younger man's cock twitched beneath his stained jeans. "I can think of a few things, sweetheart."

"A bit more meat on your bones and I could think of a few things myself," the older man drawled thickly, his hand now rubbing the bulge in his black jeans.

She couldn't stop a shudder of revulsion. She only hoped her small breasts kept them distracted. As their gaze fastened onto her rounded globes she wet her lips and channeled her inner wolf. "I might not have many curves, but I've had no complaints with the ones I do have."

She'd been starved of affection, starved of love and dignity. Little wonder she'd had no appetite. But no more. Thanks to Dane, now the real Elyse was back and hungry for life.

She could see Dane's werewolf form metamorphosing into human. The hunters wouldn't notice, distracted as they were by her breasts. She swallowed and held herself back from rushing to Dane's side, ensuring he was okay. Instead she folded her arms across her chest. "You know, I don't think Dane would be happy with you two right now."

The men looked at one another, their lust-filled grins diminishing at a rate of knots. "Dane...Dane Maddox?" the younger man asked uncertainly. "You're his woman?"

Behind them, Dane climbed onto his feet with silent stealth, the streams of blood drying on his chest, the ripples of his abs somehow emphasizing the dark fury written all over his face. He moved between the two men, standing in front of Elyse and shielding her from their lewd stares.

He turned to her with a bemused smile. "So that's where you got to, my darling. Next time you want to make love under the trees and then expect me to give chase, at least give me a clue what direction you're heading!"

He faced the hunters, his smile touched with ice. "I ever hear you men offending my woman, I ever see either one of you step foot on my property again, and I will personally see you live to regret it."

The emphasis he put on "live" had a little shiver brush over her body. Dane wouldn't be above a spot of torture if the need arose. And in that moment she understood he'd seen and done far worse in his long life.

The hunters' faces blanched. The younger man blabbered, "Sorry, Mr. Maddox. We were just having some fun. No harm intended."

The older man interrupted, explaining, "We were told a big black dog roamed this part of the bush and if we shot and killed it, we'd be paid big money."

Dane's spine stiffened. "Is that so?" he said quietly. "On my land?"

The young hunter pulled a silver bullet from his pocket. "Yes." He nodded his head, as if imparting this knowledge would make things right. "We were told to use this to finish the job."

Elyse closed her eyes. "Caleb."

Her revolting ex had clearly had a back-up plan if all else failed. The men shuffled backward, the eldest stuttering, "Um, if—if that's all, then we'll—we'll be leaving."

"No, that's not all," said Dane. "Tell anyone else stupid enough to look for this dog that I'll catch them and it will be their name on the silver bullet."

Almost falling over each other, the hunters turned tail and ran—apparently not even noticing that very dog had disappeared.

Dane turned to her and she fell into his arms, gasping and choking on tears. "I thought I'd lost you!"

"No," he soothed. "They didn't get to use the silver bullet. I was never going to go away that easily." A smile warmed his voice. "If plan A didn't work for Caleb, plan B didn't stand half a chance. He won't bother us again. I think his hands will be full now."

A picture of the catlike brown-haired girl intruded. She nodded, relaxing in his arms. She looked up, into his loving stare. "Can we go to the cabin now?" she said huskily. "Just for the night. It feels right, somehow."

He nodded, one hand stroking back her wet hair, the other hand smoothing her tears dry, his expression so tender her chest ached with need...with love. "If that's what you want."

When she nodded, he said huskily, "Happy birthday, Elyse." Her eyes misted, and it had little to do with the rain. "Thank you."

Thunder clapped in the distance, but she was almost oblivious to everything but Dane. It was impossible now to contemplate a life without him. Impossible to imagine being with anyone else.

By the time they made it to the cabin, thrusting the door open with a bang, they were already in each other's arms, hungrily kissing. Elyse was half-mad with need for him, and by the growl tearing from his throat, the press of his rock-hard cock against her belly, the feeling was mutual.

He propelled her backward until her shoulders thumped against the wall, one of his big hands spreading apart the flesh of her wet cunt before one finger, then two, slid deep in and out.

She whimpered into his mouth as every feel-good cell in her body lit up like a sensitive length of fuse. And when his thumb found the hard nub of her clit and deftly massaged, she pulled her mouth from his and cried out his name, her legs all but giving out beneath her.

He held her easily, his eyes gleaming with carnal knowledge. Then he was turning her around and pushing her forward a couple of steps, his mouth nuzzling her throat and sending electric shivers right to her toes. "It's not over yet, my sweet," he murmured huskily. "Not by a long shot."

Then he was pressing her down until she was leaning over the rickety table on her forearms, the hard ripples of his chest and sinewy belly, the even harder length of cock, rubbing against her spine, her buttocks. She gasped as the head of his cock rubbed the entrance of her pussy, and she squirmed, wanting him so bad—

"Ahh." Dane half growled the words as the full length of his cock slid deep inside her cunt.

Elyse bit her bottom lip as new sensation rippled through her nerve endings, the pleasure almost beyond endurance. "Just fuck me," she moaned. "Fuck me hard."

He pulled out and then slammed back in, and she bucked against his hard and fast rhythm as another climax built and built. She threw her head back and closed her eyes as she came apart in delicious shockwaves of pleasure, one after the other.

Dane groaned, his seed jetting hot inside, his heart thudding hard in his chest that rose and fell against her back as he slumped against her, holding her tight. He pulled out and turned her around, scooping her into his arms and carrying her into the dank bedroom.

It didn't matter to Elyse. Right then the bedroom was fit for a queen. He laid her down and climbed onto the bed beside her, drawing her close and taking hold of her mouth with his in a slow, leisurely kiss that had her softly sighing.

"I love you," she said, holding his stare. Dane had never stalked her. He'd waited for her to come to him of her own instinctual volition. Waited for her arrival close by to this cabin, which he undoubtedly owned. And all of a sudden it made perfect sense why Caleb hated her so much, why he'd succumbed to the violence he carried within.

It was a female lycan's instinct to find their mate, but Caleb had pursued her regardless, all the while knowing she wasn't his *weren*, knowing she belonged to another. He'd admitted guessing her true mate was Dane, his hated rival.

Dane's smile was echoed in the elation glinting in his eyes. His breath fanned her cheek. "We were fated from the start, our love preordained."

She shrugged. "I'm certain I would have loved you regardless of fate's plans."

His smile widened. "I feel the same way."

She sighed and snuggled close to his warmth, the musk of their sex potent in the air. "I love you, Dane." She giggled a little. "I think I might enjoy saying that at odd moments."

"I love you too," he murmured. "My *weren* queen."

She played with the strands of his dark hair that brushed his broad shoulders, coiling them around her finger. "Queen?"

He chuckled in rich, warm tones that rippled through her like silk. "As the eldest, strongest alpha male, I'm lycan king." He shuffled down a little, kissing the shell of her ear. "If it pleases you, in the morning, we'll go to the main house and I'll cook you up a feast fit for a *weren* queen."

She smiled up at him, feeling freer and happier than what she had in a very long time. There would be plenty time for introspection, for questions, later. Going up on tiptoe, she kissed him hard. The inner fire had been banked, burning now with little restraint. When she stepped back, she said with a bold grin, "For the first time in years I feel ravenous with hunger."

His gray eyes gleamed silver. "That sounds promising." She stretched, then pushed him onto his back. She climbed on top, her breasts already hardening beneath his heated stare. "I do believe I've found my soul mate."

Want more exciting, award winning paranormal stories from Mel Teshco...
Shadow Hunter - a full length novel

Being a Shadow Hunter is everything to Kyra. It gives her the right to exterminate those hybrids who are a bane to every purebred vampire and werewolf in existence. That her next mission is to finally take away the life of her maker, Altair, the same man who was once a mighty vampire who'd changed her and made her his wife, is nothing more than a happy coincidence.

Until she realizes their chemistry is far from done and he has risked everything to make her his again. It's her aversion to drinking blood that leaves her vulnerable to him, and suddenly he's tipped her world upside down again and they are on the run together from the very Shadow Hunters who'd once been her comrades.

But Altair isn't the only man willing to be her protector, and in the end only one thing matters. Will she follow her head, or her heart?

Chapter One of Shadow Hunter

Kyra Delano sipped from her glass of whiskey on the rocks, savoring the sharp burn on her tongue and the chill of ice melting in its wake.

The heady fumes assailed her acute sense of smell and removed her for a moment from stale cigarette smoke, old beer spills and sweat—a prerequisite for every Sydney nightclub she'd visited this last month.

She took another sip of whiskey, but this time it failed to ease the tension within. She shouldn't be here. The risk was too high. She broke every shadow hunter rule by coming into the nightclub when she should be waiting outside in the darkness, hidden and ready to attack.

She stared into the mirrored wall behind the bar, which displayed the dance floor and the crowd of gyrating humans. All her instincts jangled alert. She'd stay a few minutes more. Her target was here. She just needed to wait it out.

Then she'd give into her bloodlust.

A figure in the crowd caught her eye. Her senses sharpened.

Altair Delano.

Not exactly the monster she had hoped to eliminate, despite his changed DNA.

Her fingers clenched before she tossed back the remainder of her drink and slammed it onto the pitted bar. She turned in her spiked, knee-high boots to face the dance floor.

Striding forward, she brushed past a smooth, suit-and-tie man who'd wasted his breath the last ten minutes with his unoriginal pick-up lines. She smiled without humor. Another time, another place, perhaps she'd have taken advantage of his interest and overcome her unnatural aversion to drinking blood.

Except that would also mean the possibility of surrendering to her vampire needs and fucking the human too, and that was the one thing she just couldn't do. Had never done. Sucking blood and sex might go hand-in-hand, but she'd never been like other vampires and she wasn't about to start now.

Rock music jarred her sensitive ears and light strobes dazzled her vision as she pushed her way through the dancing throng, but her attention remained on her target.

He all but lounged against the far wall, a svelte blonde woman pressed against him. A large splayed hand rested on the woman's bared waist as she stood on tiptoe, trailing kisses across the base of his throat, her fingers twined through his rumpled, midnight hair.

His head lifted, his brilliant stare pinpointing Kyra before a smile spread across his beautiful face. A face she'd once thought she'd known so well.

Her eyes narrowed even as all breath stilled in her lungs. Altair was no longer her husband, her mate. He'd discarded her. Abandoned and betrayed her. All he was to her now was her next mission.

The music abruptly changed. She paused, then raised her arms and tossed back her head to expose her throat. Her tied-back, ebony hair brushed past her waist as she slowly swiveled her hips with instinctive, sensual moves that Altair would be unable to ignore.

Her eyes met his glowing amber stare.

If you want me, come and get me.

She arched her spine, her hands drifting past her tight midriff top and across her bared belly as her hips continued to undulate to the pulsing sound. The tempo increased. Bass and drums swelled until an orchestra, unexpected and violent, pulsed with its own brand of passion.

Kyra allowed the music to engulf her, become part of her psyche. Altair would be compelled to join her, to dance with the woman who'd once been his mate.

She sensed his approach even before one of his hands seized her upper arm, pulling her against him.

"It's been too long, my love," his velvet voice purred against her ear.

Two years, one month and three days, you bastard! But who's counting?

His thumbs caressed the smooth line of her barely there leather miniskirt. "Outrageous as always," Altair said with a satisfied smirk. "But then, have you ever worn panties?"

"Cumbersome things, don't you think?" She kept her voice light, halted a purr of rapture at his closeness even as her gut twisted as though a knot.

Definitely not a monster...not yet.

He was a mastermind at reading people, but if he was aware of her mixed emotions he didn't let on. Instead he took charge on the floor, their bodies swaying with timed, sinuous grace.

She swallowed a curse, hating that he still had the power to affect her. Her pulse raced, her body trembling as his hands dropped lower still and cupped her leather-clad backside.

"If you say so," he said huskily, his brilliant stare alight with intelligence and unconcealed obsession. "Either that or it's my lucky day."

He dipped her back before she could make a scathing reply, her hair brushing the floor when he swept her into a semi-circle before drawing her erect, their faces inches apart.

"Actually, I think your luck just ran out," she hissed, then immediately swallowed a groan as he jerked her snug against him. His arousal strained against her exposed belly, his faint notes of citrus spice teasing her senses and causing her incisors to emerge.

He arched a dark brow. "I'm a predator like you, the top of the food chain." His breath teased her ear. "I'm not that easy to execute."

He was her physical superior and they both knew it.

His smile broadened into a lazy grin, revealing his own elongated, razor sharp fangs. "I'd have been slain long ago if not for my skills."

Aikido, judo, Kendo, Ninjutsu. He'd studied them all and more, and taught her much of his expertise.

She stiffened in his arms, fascination eroding back into contempt as the still-fresh memories of his desertion surfaced. "I've no doubt about that," she said coldly. "But it's an ability you've exploited for your own end."

His smile turned mocking. "You prefer that I take only the will of humans who abuse life? Murderers, rapists..."

His derision was infuriating. Altair knew full well she referred to his werewolf genetics that he'd acquired by force. He'd overcome his werewolf opponent, then drank its blood and became something...more. Something powerful and dangerous that would eventually see him become an indiscriminate, cold-blooded killer.

Something that as a shadow hunter she had to eliminate at all costs.

"No, that's the last thing I'd expect," she said. "I know your fascination with innocence." She was living proof. Once she'd been a mortal, a woman with hopes and dreams to spare.

His hands tightened, his grip almost cruel. "You ridicule what we had." He bent forward, his breath once again caressing her ear. "I was addicted to everything about you—your virtue—your beauty. Hell, even your revulsion to drinking blood."

"Then at least one thing hasn't changed." She raked a hand down the side of his neck, her long red fingernails drawing beads of crimson. She leaned in close, doing her best not to inhale. "Although the temptation to drink grows day-by-day, I'd die before tasting even one drop of blood from you."

He sucked in a breath even as he scrutinized her face.

She stepped away, her hands fisting at her sides. Who was she trying to kid? The fresh scent of him was nearly her undoing. Her whole system cried out to sink her fangs into his throat, to take what she knew he'd offer.

"Scared, Kyra?"

"You're a hybrid," she spat. "Your very existence spells death to the vampire race—all the secret races."

The scratches along his neck had almost closed, a bright spatter of crimson the only evidence that she'd touched him, hurt him. She held back a groan. She wanted only to lean forward and lick clean his throat, taste his life essence.

His mouth hardened. "You wouldn't believe such untruths if you'd take the time to research our way of life...our evolution."

All hunger fled as she suppressed a shudder of revulsion. Just how many of his kind were there? "I'll send you to hell first," she snarled. Except the bastard knew only too well she wouldn't fight him here, not with a nightclub full of human witnesses.

He moved forward, his eyes unreadable as he lifted a hand to brush his knuckles in a sensual trail along her cheek. He smiled a little at her involuntary shiver. "Then I guess I'll be seeing you again soon."

She jerked back. "Count on it."

Cold air hit Kyra when she pushed through the doors, her boots clattering on the well-lit pavement. She breathed deep of the arctic air, reveling in the bite of winter as passers-by shrugged into their jackets and tugged their scarves close, their breaths clouding before them like smoke.

It had been almost two decades since she'd suffered the frigid sting of a winter's breath. Two decades since she'd unknowingly drank Altair's blood and became vampire.

His queen.

She had one thing to thank Altair for, Kyra acknowledged with a bitter-sweet pang. She felt little physical discomfort and was blessed with great strength, well-being, and a brilliant mind. But immortality would have to be the ultimate prize.

Striding along the sidewalk, she lifted a hand to repel the bright streetlamps from her eyes while reaching into the inner pocket of her skirt to retrieve dark-tinted sunglasses.

Only after she'd veered into a dark side street did she feel secure, her hand dropping as she lifted her face to absorb the shadowy atmosphere.

Soon, it would be dawn.

Sudden longing swept over her. A profound ache at the almost forgotten familiarity of the sun on her face, its warmth caressing her skin as light spilled across lush green countryside, or glinted over deep azure ocean waves.

With a sigh, she pushed her sunglasses firmly into place and strode onward, paying little heed to the hollow-eyed whores staking out their territory along the seedier part of Sydney's, King's Cross.

Harder to ignore was the deep hunger inside, the insatiable need to feed. And the knowledge many of these women wouldn't deny her hunger or show any resistance.

She ignored the demands of her body again. But knew she couldn't hold out much longer. Either she obtained imitation hemoglobin, or she'd have no choice but to feed from a mortal.

Her lip curled. A vampire's one weakness was the need for human blood. Drink or die. It was intolerable that even the thought of taking from a mortal could make her feel so wretched and ashamed—and at the height of bloodlust—so utterly euphoric. She was only glad she'd never given into her sexual appetites with a human...it was the one thing she had above all other vampires.

If only wished an animal's blood sufficed. But it didn't. It was akin to a human existing on a diet of different flavored lollipops, edible perhaps once or twice, but sickly-tasting and without nutrition long term.

Twin columns that were patchy and graying with age fronted the flight of stairs that Kyra took to the motel room she'd paid for in advance.

The vampire council had given her three more days to defeat the hybrid who'd flaunted age-old conventions for his own wicked purpose. She gritted her teeth. She could have killed Altair once and for all tonight if she hadn't let her human side overrule her vampire side. But the moment she'd closed in on him she'd wanted to observe him first, wanted to see if he really had changed.

He hadn't. He was still the same arrogant and beautiful creature she'd met and fell in love with all those years ago. But then he'd turned her love into hate and her heart into stone. Shame she'd forgotten all that when he'd drawn her into his arms on the dance floor...

Kyra paused outside her room, pushing all thoughts of Altair away as she listened for motion and scented for any intrusion. Even shadow hunters had non-human enemies. She snorted. "Who am I kidding," she muttered. "I'd probably be too weak now to fend off even a mortal."

Like it or not, she'd have to feed after waking to the new night.

She stepped inside, a quick glance taking in the hovel she temporarily called home. An old double bed with sagging springs and a faded bed cover competed for space with a small round table and two metal chairs. A bar fridge crouched between a sink with a dripping tap and the kitchenette's roach-ridden pantry.

Her lips twitched into a smile. It wasn't exactly the Hilton, but cheap accommodation meant she could lay low and unobtrusive, mix with the underworld crowd who were in the know.

She flicked on the dullest light, giving the outward appearance of being normal, human. Tossing her sunglasses onto the table, she stripped as she made her way to the bed, naked then except for her knee-high boots with their concealed, custom-fitted weapons. Her arsenal was always the last to be shed.

Sinking onto the edge of the mattress, she paused. She could feel the morning's arrival in her bones like a deep, nagging ache. But it didn't quite shake a vague sense of unease.

Once the sun fully cleared the horizon she'd be compelled to sleep. It was a vampire's biggest weakness, a drawback that was emphasized right then by her buzzing senses. In perhaps ten minutes or so she'd be comatose and about as useless as a babe in a cot.

With a smooth motion she freed her favorite dagger from the scabbard inside her left boot. Its curved handle had become a near seamless extension in her grasp, but she took care in handling the razor-sharp blade that'd been etched with silver.

In her present condition, just one scratch and she'd be holed-up for a week. Time enough to suffer a long and torturous death as her need for human blood peaked. She wasn't about to be reduced to little more than a mound of dust.

Kyra's pulse quickened, her skin prickling with sensation.

Someone approached, a male whose scent of testosterone breached her guard long before she made out the slow beat of his heart, his steady breathing as he climbed the stairs, silent as a specter.

An immortal.

Adrenalin surged as she slipped from the bed, the air around her barely stirring as she crouched low, adopting a loose-limbed position. Clasping her dagger, she raised her left arm, her lips pulling into a grimace as her belly shrieked feral hunger.

The doorknob twisted. She launched her knife just as Altair emerged, all broad shoulders and looming height. Neatly sidestepping, he plucked the weapon from midair—as if it was a mere irritation—a mosquito.

"You!" she hissed. Dear God. She must be weaker than she'd thought. How could her senses have let her down by not identifying him? She exhaled with disgust, hating him, but hating even more the tug of yearning within.

"You disappoint me." He clucked his tongue as she stood. "I expected an element of surprise."

She refused to respond, refused to even budge as he flicked off the light and moved forward, stalking his prey.

"Perhaps it would've been easier to take me to bed first?" he asked with a growl. "Entertain me before plunging your pretty knife into my heart?"

Unease escalated, nausea climbing up her throat. She stifled a sharp intake of breath as Altair flung the dagger forward. The gust of its momentum brushed her cheek before it buried up to the hilt in the wall behind her.

He took hold of her upper arms and pressed her backward. "Except you're not quite that desperate," he growled, his white fangs evident as he lowered his head, his breath fanning her ear, "your lack of nourishment not yet clouding your judgment, hmm?"

Her skin shivered with his touch, his familiarity, and adrenalin bolted through her blood like a junkie's re-awakened craving. She wanted him inside her, filling her slowly as he watched the expressions chase over her face...

No!

Kyra stepped away, launching a right and then left punch. But he deflected the blows with ease, until she pretended to spin and then smashed a knee into his groin.

He doubled over with a grunt, and she vaulted onto the bed, aware of his quick recovery even before she turned to face him.

She trailed her knuckles along the underside of her breasts. "I think you're too easily distracted." Her lips quirked. "You've lost your edge."

His eyes smoldered into iridescent yellow as they followed her hands. When he leaped, she flipped backwards and dropped lightly onto her feet, her palms raised and inwardly turned.

"I'm getting to you," she taunted.

His mouth tilted into a smile that didn't make it to his eyes. "Some things never change."

And yet you gave it all away.

Her voice chilled. "It must be hell to want someone you can no longer have?"

His gaze dropped and the temperature soared as his stare leisurely stroked over every dip and curve of her body. Her nipples puckered, heat flooding her core. He smirked. "I could take you now and you wouldn't have the will to fight me."

Her chin kicked up. "I came here to kill you, not to fuck."

He arched a dark brow. "But fucking is much more fun, don't you think?"

Memories flooded her mind. Their bodies twisted together as one, their moans piercing the air while their pleasure intensified...

Sudden white-hot pain twisted inside her guts and shot through her veins like a corkscrew, dispersing all thought. She gasped, doubling over as waves of agony pierced her skull and reverberated through her bones.

Dawn had arrived.

For your exclusive FREE story: Her Dark Guardian, and where you can find out when my next book is available, as well as other news, cover reveals and more, sign up for my newsletter: https://madmimi.com/signups/121695/join

Check out my website – http://www.melteshco.com/

You can also friend me on Facebook at https://www.facebook.com/mel.teshco

Or my author Facebook page at https://www.facebook.com/MelTeshcoAuthor

And occasionally on Twitter at https://twitter.com/melteshco

Contact me: melteshco@yahoo.com.au

If you enjoy my books I'd be delighted if you would consider leaving a review. This will help other readers find my books ☺

About the Author

Mel Teshco loves to write scorching hot sci-fi and contemporary stories with an occasional paranormal thrown into the mix. Not easy with seven cats, two dogs and a fat black thoroughbred vying for attention, especially when Mel's also busily stuffing around on Facebook. With only one daughter now living at home to feed two minute noodles, she still shakes her head at how she managed to write with three daughters and three stepchildren living under the same roof. Not to mention Mr. Semi-Patient (the one and same husband hoping for early retirement...he's been waiting a few years now.) Clearly anything is possible, even in the real world.

Want more Mel Teshco books?
Science Fiction:
The Virgin Hunt Games:
The Virgin Hunt Games volume 1
The Virgin Hunt Games volume 2
The Virgin Hunt Games volume 3
The Virgin Hunt Games volume 4
The Virgin Hunt Games volume 5
The Virgin Hunt Games volume 6
Dragons of Riddich:
Kadin (prequel - book 1)
Asher (book 2)
Baron (book 3)
Dahlia (book 4)
Wyatt (book 5)
Valor (book 6)
The Queen (book 7)
Alien Fugitives:
Nero (book 1)
Jasper (book 2)
Sienna (book 3)
Damaris (book 4)
Zander (book 5)
Jaire (book 6)
Epello (book 7)
Alien Hunger:
Galactic Burn (book 1)
Galactic Inferno (book 2)
Galactic Flame (book 3)
Coming soon
Galactic Blaze (book 4)
Nightmix:

Lusting the Enemy (book 1)
Abducting the Princess (book 2)
Seducing the Huntress (book 3)
Winged & Dangerous:
Stone Cold Lover (book 1)
Ice Cold Lover (book 2)
Red Hot Lover (book 3)
Winged & Dangerous Box Set (all 3 books in the series)
Dirty Sexy Space continuity with authors Shona Husk and Denise Rossetti:
Yours to Uncover (book 1)
Mine to Serve (book 6)
Ours to Share (book 8)
Awakenings series with Kylie Sheaffe
No Ordinary Gift (book 1)
Believe (book 2)
Homecoming (book 3)
Standalone longer length titles: (50k-100k)
Dimensional
Mutant Unveiled
Shadow Hunter
Existence
Standalone novellas and short stories: (15k-40K)
Identity Shift
Moon Thrall
Blood Chance
Carnal Moon
Contemporary:
Desert Kings Alliance:
The Sheikh's Runaway Bride (book 1)
The Sheikh's Captive Lover (book 2)
The Sheikh's Forbidden Wife (book 3)

The Sheikh's Secret Mistress (book 4)
The Sheikh's Defiant Princess (book 5)
The Sheikh's Fake Fiancée (book 6)
The Sheikh's Royal Widow (book 7)
The VIP Desire Agency
Lady in Red (book 1)
High Class (book 2)
Exclusive (book 3)
Liberated (book 4)
Uninhibited (book 5)
The VIP Desire Agency Boxed Set (all 5 books in the series)
Box sets with authors Christina Phillips & Cathleen Ross
Sheikhs & Billionaires
Taken by the Sheikh
Taken by the Billionaire
Taken by the Desert Sheikh
Resisting the Firefighter
Standalone longer length titles: (50k-100k)
Highest Bid
As I Am
Standalone novellas and short stories: (15k-40K)
Stripped
Clarissa
Camilla
Selena's Bodyguard (also part of the Christmas Assortment Box)\
Anthologies:
Down and Dusty: The Complete Collection
The Christmas Assortment Box
Secret Confessions: Sydney Housewives

www.ingramcontent.com/pod-product-compliance
Lightning Source LLC
Chambersburg PA
CBHW031500130726
47989CB00003B/1477